is the B

Val Biro

Published by the Penguin Group
Penguin Books Ltd, 27 Wrights Lane, London
W8 5TZ, England
Penguin Books Australia Ltd, Ringwood,
Victoria, Australia
Penguin Books Canada Ltd, 10 Alcorn Avenue,
Toronto, Ontario, Canada M4V 3B2
Penguin Books (NZ) Ltd, 182-190 Wairau Road,
Auckland 10, New Zealand

Penguin Books Ltd, Registered Offices:
Harmondsworth, Middlesex, England

This edition first published in Great Britain in 1984
by Hodder and Stoughton

This edition published by Claremont Books,
an imprint of Godfrey Cave Associates Limited,
42 Bloomsbury Street, London, WC1B 3QJ,
under licence from Val Biro, 1996

Copyright © 1984 Val Biro

ISBN 1 854 71796 0

Mr Josiah Oldcastle was very fond of Gumdrop. It was a vintage car with proper mudguards and running-boards, and it had lamps and horn and radiator, all in brass.

It was old, of course, but then Mr Oldcastle didn't like new cars anyway. It wasn't very fast and it had no modern gadgets, but Mr Oldcastle didn't mind at all. To him, Gumdrop was beautiful, safe, sensible and strong. In short, it was the best car, and better than most.

But some other drivers felt differently. There was Mr Uppety Upstart, for instance, who had a brand-new car.

'It's about time you scrapped that old heap of yours,' he said. 'Look at it! No automatics, no electronics, no gadgets. What a useless old crock!'

But Mr Oldcastle said nothing, because he knew better.

Or take young Snippety Whippet who
had a sports-car.

'My car is faster than yours,' he boasted.
'And no wonder! I bet those clumsy big
wheels of yours can hardly turn round!'
But Mr Oldcastle just smiled and said
nothing.

Then there was Mrs Penny Pincher who had a small car.

'I can't imagine how you can afford to run such a heavy old car. It must use gallons of petrol.' She looked very smug. 'My little car is so economical that it hardly uses any!'
Mr Oldcastle said nothing, but smiled politely.

Now it so happened that he went on a long journey one day. Driving along a lonely country road he saw a small car standing in the way. And its driver was none other than Mrs Pincher.

'I've run out of petrol,' she wailed, 'and there isn't a garage for miles!' She looked most upset.

'Allow me to help, madam,' said Mr Oldcastle as he unbolted Gumdrop's spare petrol can on the running-board. He poured the fuel into the little car's tank.

Mrs Pincher was very grateful. 'How sensible it is to carry spare petrol like that,' she said. 'I must say that Gumdrop is the best car after all.'

Mr Oldcastle bowed politely. 'And better than most,' he said.

A few days later Mr Oldcastle went to visit a castle. As he parked Gumdrop in a nearby field he noticed that a sports-car was trying to leave.

But its small wheels were spinning round on the wet grass and digging themselves into the mud. The car was unable to move. Its driver was young Snippety Whippet who looked most upset.

'Allow me to help,' said Mr Oldcastle. He tied a tow-rope to the sports-car and Gumdrop pulled it slowly and surely out of the mud. Young Snippety was very grateful.

'Fancy that! I did not realise how strong those big wheels were. They'd grip on any slippery surface! I must say that Gumdrop is the best car after all.'

'Yes,' agreed Mr Oldcastle with a nod, 'and better than most.'

When he came out of the castle, Mr Oldcastle noticed a big commotion in the field. Everybody was running about and shouting.

And no wonder, because a brand-new car was on fire! Its electronics must have got into a twist. People tried to put it out by blowing and fanning, which of course made it much worse.

'Allow me to help,' said Mr Oldcastle and he ran to Gumdrop. He whipped out the brass fire-extinguisher, pointed it at the flames and put the fire out in no time. Everybody cheered his brave and swift action.

'Well done!' exclaimed Mr Uppety Upstart who owned the car.
'With all my electronics and gadgets, yours is a much safer car, because it carries a fire-extinguisher. I must say that Gumdrop is the best car after all.'

Mr Oldcastle clamped the extinguisher back on the running-board, got into Gumdrop and started the engine. He smiled at Mr Upstart. 'Yes,' he said 'and better than most.' With which he waved at one and all and drove home.